THE QUEEN WHO STOLE THE SKY

by Jennifer Garrett
illustrated by Linda Hendry

Scholastic-TAB Publications Ltd.,
123 Newkirk Road, Richmond Hill, Ontario, Canada

Canadian Cataloguing in Publication Data
Garrett, Jennifer.
  The Queen who stole the sky
ISBN 0-590-71524-0 (bound). — ISBN 0-590-71523-2 (pbk.)
I. Hendry, Linda. II. Title.
PZ7.G376Qu 1986   j823'.914   C85-098478-5

876543   Printed in Hong Kong   9/801234/9

The village of Bamble was small and poor. A stranger passing through might not have noticed it at all if it hadn't been for the enormous marble castle standing by the river. This was the home of Queen Tallyrat.

A vainer queen had never lived. The castle walls were covered in mirrors, and Queen Tallyrat needed a hundred polishers just to keep them shiny. She spent all her time changing dresses and admiring herself.

To pay for her huge wardrobe, she taxed the people of Bamble so heavily they could barely afford to eat.

She taxed their walls, their shoes and their kettles. She taxed their doors, their doorknobs and their chairs. Once, she taxed everything beginning with *t* — trousers, tables, even Tuesdays!

The Queen's personal servants, Fergus and Spike, followed her everywhere. They kissed the hem of her dress as she walked and called her "The Splendour of Bamble" and "Our Most Wondrous and Stunning Queen." But to each other they called her "Old Hippo Face" and "Crowbrain."

On the other side of the river, at the edge of Farmer Tuck's field, stood a tumbledown shack. This was the home of the Plunkett family. Mrs. Plunkett was sickly and frail, and the musty cottage air seemed to make her grow sicker by the day. She had nothing to feed her seven children, and every morning they walked to the village to beg for food.

All except Tabatha, that is. Tabatha had long red hair she seldom combed, and so many freckles that the people in the village called her "Pepperface." She didn't worry. She just shrugged her shoulders and looked for some mischief to get into. She loved to knock on doors and run away, or drop chestnuts onto the bald heads of men passing by.

"That girl will be the death of me," her mother often said.

In the evenings, while her brothers and sisters huddled round the tiny fire, Tabatha paraded up and down in funny clothes. She imitated farmer Tuck in his big clumsy boots, and the Mayor in his ginger wig. But her imitation of Queen Tallyrat was best of all. She would dress up in a potato sack and strut around the room admiring herself in an imaginary mirror, until her family roared with laughter and forgot how hungry they were.

The only pleasure the villagers had was at harvest festival time. Although they were not invited to the Royal Ball, everyone joined in the excitement. The marble castle was polished and the streets were cleaned. Food of every sort was prepared and decorations were hung. Even the Plunketts' little shack was covered with dried flowers and coloured rags.

As the day of the ball approached, Queen Tallyrat looked through her immense wardrobe. She tried on gown after gown, each more lovely than the last. But every one she cast aside. "Queen Bella will be there in her fabulous dress of woven emeralds," she wailed, throwing a shoe at Spike. "What if people think she is more beautiful than I am?"

"How is that possible, Your Loveliness?" replied Spike. "You are the most beautiful queen in the universe." But under his breath he added "Donkeypuss."

More than anything Queen Tallyrat wanted to outdo Queen Bella. She summoned her tailor. "Make me a dress so magnificent I will be the talk of the land," she commanded.

The next day he came in holding a dazzling gown made of hummingbird feathers and ruby dust. She frowned and sent him to make another. Many lovely dresses followed, some woven from the finest Persian silks, some embroidered with unicorn hair. But none pleased her.

The Queen flew into a rage. She doubled everyone's taxes. She threw her tailor and all her dressmakers into the dungeon. Even Fergus and Spike did not dare go near her.

The day before the ball, Queen Tallyrat stood frowning out the window. She was gazing absently at the spectacular sunset when suddenly she had an idea — a perfectly wonderful idea!

"Fergus! Spike! Come here!" she screamed. They both came running, covering their heads for fear she would throw something at them. "Summon my tailor and my dressmakers from the dungeons," she ordered.

When they were all kneeling in front of her, she announced grandly, "I have decided what I want to wear to the ball."

"What is it, Your Majesty?" asked the tailor.

"The *sky*," she said, pointing out the window. "I want a dress made out of the sky."

"The sky!" said Fergus in a tiny voice.

"The sky?" said Spike, in an even tinier voice.

"That's right," said the Queen, her eyes flashing.

No one moved. They looked at her. She looked at them. Finally she stamped her foot. *"Now!"*

The tailor and the dressmakers scrambled to their feet, tripping over each other in their haste. Off they marched to the edge of the sky, armed with scissors, clippers and shears. Immediately they began pulling and cutting, pulling and cutting.

Tabatha was in Farmer Tuck's field, chasing his cows, when she noticed a crowd forming nearby. She ran over to have a look. "What's going on?" she asked.

No one answered. They couldn't imagine what the tailor and the dressmakers were doing. Then all of a sudden Tabatha realized what was happening.

"They're stealing the sky!" she cried, rushing at them and pelting them with stones. It made no difference.

Rrriippp! With a great tearing sound, the final edge tore away, and the tailor and the dressmakers ran back to the castle clutching the sky. It billowed and flew about their heads like a gigantic blanket caught in the wind.

They worked all night and all the next day, measuring and cutting, stitching and hemming. Just before sunset they marched into the Queen's chamber with the finished dress. For once in her life, Queen Tallyrat smiled.

"Help me!" she cried, nearly ripping the dress in her eagerness to put it on.

As she turned to look at herself in the mirror, a soft lilac light filled the room. The dress quivered and shone. It was pale violet with tiny white clouds floating around the sleeves and a soft amber haze circling the hem. Soon the violet turned to mauve, and the clouds gathered around the waist in a fiery fuchsia band. As sunset moved into evening, the skirt blazed with gold and scarlet streaks, fading into a bodice of sapphire.

At last the hour of the
ball arrived. Crouched in
the branches of a huge oak tree,
Tabatha watched the lords and ladies
alight from their coaches. They were
dressed in gowns made of silver and
satin, capes woven from panther tails,
and robes studded with aquamarines.
Inside the palace she could see tables laden
with food — platters of steaming roast dragon
in pepper sauce, bowls of giant apricots, goblets
of sweet lotus nectar. The air was filled with music
and laughter.

At the head of the stairs, seven pages in burgundy tunics raised their trumpets and sounded a fanfare. After a long moment of silence, Queen Tallyrat appeared. The dress was now a deep midnight blue, covered in tiny stars that sparkled and shimmered and outshone the lanterns on the walls. A gasp of amazement swept through the room.

As she slowly descended the staircase, some of the stars shot off the dress, setting fire to the carpet. Fergus and Spike ran behind, stamping out the flames.

Queen Tallyrat, her head high, moved toward the dance floor. She made sure she passed close to Queen Bella, whose face turned a delightful, envious green — almost the same shade as her emerald dress.

All night the Queen waltzed with lords and dukes and kings, while everyone stared in wonder at her magical dress. Looking on, Tabatha seethed with fury. How dare the Queen be so gay! How dare she feast on exotic delicacies while Tabatha's family went hungry! How dare she steal the sky!

After the ball, Queen Tallyrat danced all the way to her room, trailing stars behind her. She fell asleep just as dawn was beginning to appear around the hem of her gown.

When she awoke, her tailor and all her dressmakers were standing anxiously around her.

"What is it?" she asked, yawning.

"Is Your Majesty going to take the dress off now?" asked the tailor.

"Why should I?"

"The humble people of Bamble have requested that you put the sky back where it belongs."

"*What?*" she shrieked. "How dare they! I shall take it off when I please!"

"Perhaps, Most Gracious of All Queens, you should take it off so it can be ironed," Spike suggested.

"*Never!*" she cried. "I shall never take it off!"

Weeks went by and the people of Bamble grew more and more desperate. Not only were they poor, now they had no sky to look at. There was just an empty grey hole where it used to be. At night there were no stars to wish upon. There was no rain to water the fields. Soon all the crops died and all the rivers and lakes dried up. Never before had there been such famine.

But Queen Tallyrat would not give up her dress. She loved standing in front of her mirrors, watching it change colours. Sometimes it was covered with dapple-grey clouds, and other times it was a clear summer blue.

A state of emergency was declared. The Mayor offered one thousand gold pieces to any person who could retrieve the sky. People came from far and wide to earn the reward. Some tried to steal the sky while the Queen slept. Others tried to bribe her with promises of an even better dress. But no one succeeded.

One morning Tabatha woke up to find her brothers and sisters weak from hunger, and her mother too ill to get out of bed. Without the sky, the days were drab and colourless, and not even Tabatha could make them smile.

"Come on," she said. "It's not so bad. We'll move to a nice forest where things are clean and beautiful." She took a big book down from the shelf and began flipping through the pages to show them where they could go. Suddenly she stopped. On one page were pictures of a country where no rain had fallen for many years. The people were dressed in colourful costumes, dancing to bring rain. She had an idea, and the more she thought about it, the more she liked it. With a hoot of laughter, she leapt up and ran outside.

"I'll make Queen Tallyrat wish she had never touched the sky!" she chortled.

First she went to Farmer Tuck's farm and collected some turkey feathers and coal. She drew dark streaks on her face and stuck the feathers in her hair. Then she hurried across the bridge to the oak tree that hung over the castle moat. She scrambled up and carefully crawled along one of the branches until she reached a ledge on the castle wall. From there she climbed up to the balcony outside the Queen's window.

She peered in and saw the Queen, as usual, admiring herself in a mirror. Slowly, then faster, Tabatha began hopping from one foot to another, chanting and whirling and shaking her fists in the air.

Suddenly Queen Tallyrat noticed that her dress was changing from pink to grey, and that black swirls of cloud were forming at the edges of the hem. "What an awful colour!" she exclaimed. The skirt kept getting darker and darker until it was the shade of slate. A deep rumble sounded around her ankles.

The Queen's shriek startled Fergus and Spike. When they ran in, they found tiny spears of lightning leaping all around her. Rain was pouring from the dress, and the room was filled with water. As they floated by the windowsill, they noticed a small girl with tangled red hair gleefully dancing up and down on the balcony.

Terrified, Queen Tallyrat ripped the dress off and threw it out the window. *Whoosh.* It caught the wind and flew across the fields, billowing and ballooning like a ship's sail. It drifted upward and spread out over the land like a giant circus tent.

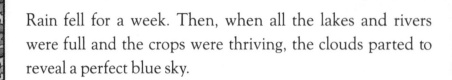

Rain fell for a week. Then, when all the lakes and rivers were full and the crops were thriving, the clouds parted to reveal a perfect blue sky.

The people of Bamble danced and sang in the streets. A crowd assembled in the square to watch the Mayor give Tabatha the thousand gold pieces. "Hooray for Tabatha!" they cheered. "Hooray for Pepperface!"

The very next day the Plunketts moved to a large, airy house on top of a hill. Mrs. Plunkett grew stronger each day, and Tabatha's brothers and sisters never had to beg again.